FIRST GRADERS from MARS

EASY

Episode 3:
Nergal and
the Great Space Race

Story by SHANA COREY
Pictures by MARK TEAGUE

SCHOLASTIC PRESS · NEW YORK

Text copyright © 2002 by Shana Corey
Illustrations copyright © 2002 by Mark Teague
All rights reserved. Published by Scholastic Press, a division of Scholastic Inc.,
Publishers since 1920. SCHOLASTIC and SCHOLASTIC PRESS and associated logos are
trademarks and/or registered trademarks of Scholastic Inc.

No part of this publication may be reproduced, or stored in a retrieval system, or transmitted in any form or
by any means, electronic, mechanical, photocopying, recording, or otherwise, without written permission
of the publisher. For information regarding permission, write to Scholastic Inc., Attention: Permissions
Department, 557 Broadway, New York, NY 10012.
Library of Congress Cataloging-in-Publication data:
Corey, Shana.
First graders from Mars episode 3: Nergal and the Great Space Race / written by Shana Corey ; illustrated
by Mark Teague.—1st ed. p.cm. Summary: When Nergal's first-grade class concentrates on health and fit-
ness during Martian Health Week, he is very nervous about doing poorly in the upcoming space race.
ISBN 0-439-26633-5
[1. Self-esteem—Fiction. 2. Racing—Fiction. 3. Extraterrestrial beings—Fiction. 4. Schools—Fiction. 5.
Mars (Planet)—Fiction.] I. Teague, Mark ill. II. Title. PZ7.C8155 F1l 2002 [E]—dc21 2001049836
10 9 8 7 6 5 4 3 2 1   02 03 04 05 06
Printed in Mexico 49
First edition, August 2002
The text type was set in 18-point Martin Gothic Medium.
Book design by Kristina Albertson

To Leslie Budnick, with thabanks. Meep! Meep!

— SC

For Zoey: Have fun in first grade!

— MT

It was the first day
of Martian Health Week.
"We will end the week with
a space race," said Ms. Vortex.
"I know we will all try
to do our martian best."

Sixteen thinking capsules
started to buzz.

"I have been waiting for this all year!" said Horus.

"Me, too," said Pelly.

"I am a wiz at the 100-meteor dash," said Tera.

Nergal was the only martian
in Pod 1 who was not
excited about the race.

Nergal remembered last year's race.

He had not done his martian best.

He had done his martian *worst*.

"Exercise is only part
of health," said Ms. Vortex.
"What we eat is also important."
She fed a rock to a plant.
The plant did a jumping jack.
"That rock had minerals," she said.
"Healthy foods give us energy."

"What about unhealthy
foods?" asked Nergal.
"Let's find out," said Ms. Vortex.
Nergal fed a nobber pop
to a plant.
The plant wilted.
Nergal knew how
it was feeling.

All week, Pod 1 learned about
health and fitness.

They learned about the 450 food groups.

They learned about balanced meals.

In the mornings,
they practiced the moon walk.
In the afternoons,
they practiced the shuttle run.

During lunch, Nergal ate an ooze-it.

Boing! Boing!

He bounced off the ceiling.

"Wabatch out," warned the lunch lady.

"Too much sugar

can make you crash!"

"Yebes," said Nergal. "I see."

Finally, it was race day.

Nergal's stomach was tied up in knots.

He raised his foot.

"Can I go see the nurse?" he asked.

"You *are* looking a little green,"

said Ms. Vortex.

"I'm sick," Nergal said.

The nurse took his temperature.

"90 below zero. You're fine," he said.

He sent Nergal back to Pod 1.

Nergal found everyone outside.

"Oh, goody!" said Pelly.

"You are just in time for the race!"

Pod 1 started to warm up.

They stretched.

They twisted.

They curled.

"The first event is the shuttle run,"
called Ms. Vortex.
Nergal's stomach dropped.
His tentacles flopped.

"On your mark, get set . . ."
Before Ms. Vortex finished,
Nergal started to run.
He ran.
And ran.
And ran.

"Where are you going?" called Pelly.
"You are running the wrong way!"
yelled Tera.
"Stop!" shouted Horus.
But Nergal didn't stop.

"Nergy! What are you doing home?"
asked Nergal's mom.
Nergal started to cry.
"I do not want to race," he sobbed.
"I am not a good runner!"
Nergal's dad gave him a hug.
"That's okay," he said.
"You are a great hopscotcher.
Nobo one's good at everything."
"You are," sniffed Nergal.

Nergal's mom started to giggle.
"What's so funny?" asked Nergal.
"I was just thinking about the time
your dad ran a three-legged race,"
said Nergal's mom.

"I was the only one with two legs,"
remembered Nergal's dad.
"Ha-ba, ha-ba, ha-ba," he laughed.
Nergal and his mom laughed, too.
"Hee-bee! Hee-bee! Hee-bee!"

"I am not a good runner either,"
said Nergal's dad.
"I guess it runs in the family."

Nergal hugged him.

"That's okay," he said.

"You are a great dad."

"I try," said Nergal's dad.

"That's what matters,"
said Nergal's mom.

Nergal's parents took him back to school.

"Nergal!" said Ms. Vortex.

"We were worried."

"I'm sorry," said Nergal.

"I am not a very good runner."

"But you ran so far!" said Horus.

"The space race is not about being good," said Ms. Vortex.

"It's about trying new things. The 100-meteor dash is next. Would you like to run, Nergal?"

Nergal looked at his podmates.
He looked at his mom and dad.
"Yebes," he said. "I'll try."
"Yabay!" everyone cheered.

Pod 1 picked up their meteors.

"On your mark, get set,

blast off!" called Ms. Vortex.

Nergal took off running.

He ran.

And ran.

And ran.

But this time, he stopped
at the finish line.
He didn't win.
But he tried his martian best.

"I'm proud of you, Pod,"
said Ms. Vortex.
"As a reward for your hard work
during Martian Health Week,
I made saucercakes."
"Yubum!" shouted Pod 1.

"I thought sweets were
bad for you," said Tera.
"Only if you overdo it,"
said Ms. Vortex.
Everyone tried a saucercake.
"Heybey," said Tera.
"These are burnt!"
"I am not a very good cook,"
admitted Ms. Vortex.

Nergal patted her arm.
"That's okay," he said.
"You are a great teacher.
What matters is you tried
your martian best."